MOS
HERE FO
SMU

MOSTLY HERE FOR THE SMUT

A READING JOURNAL

Sweet Hearts

THIS JOURNAL BELONGS TO:

CONTENTS

WELCOME 01
WHY A READING JOURNAL? 02
HOW TO USE THIS JOURNAL 04

ALL ABOUT YOU 07
YOUR READING STYLE 10
TBR (TO BE READ) 12
READING GOALS TRACKER 14
DNF (DID NOT FINISH) 16

MOSTLY HERE FOR THE SMUT 19
SMUT AND ROMANTASY 20

CONTENTS

TOP 50 ROMANTASY BOOKS 22

YOUR TOP 10 ROMANTASY BOOKS 26

READING LOG 29

ACTIVITIES 201

ALL COVERED 202

SPICE METER 206

PICK YOUR POISON 208

JUST STOP 210

BOOK CLUB CONTACT LIST 214

WELCOME

WELCOME

WHY A READING JOURNAL?

The idea of a reading journal isn't new. They've been around for about as long as books in one form or another – and for a good reason! Reading isn't passive. You'll connect with a good book, want to remember lines, people and things, which is all much easier to do if you've got something to help you. Something a little fancier and more convenient than scrawling notes in the margins.

Reading journals allow you to linger on your most recent reads, help get past the book hangover and move on to the next one. Whether you read for yourself, with friends, or in a book club, this journal is to help you put all your thoughts in order before you lose them. It can help lead you to your next great read or find the right rhythm for you to keep enjoying the books you love without letting the stressors of the real world get in the way.

Whether it's looking forward to new books to read or setting yourself some reading goals, this journal has the pages and prompts to get you going. It's important to keep a record of what you've read, to help you look back at how your personal reading went and reflect on the pages turned that you've loved. If you hit a reading slump, then working your way through the prompts on paper can help remind you what you love about reading and how to dive back into those pages.

This book may not have a convenient search function like on your screen, but there's a certain thoughtfulness that comes from putting pen to paper and making notes. You also never know what gems of the past you'll come across flicking through these pages, regardless of what you may have started searching for.

Take this journal with you whenever you take a book and the two will work together to ensure you get everything you can from every page, and the best reading experience!

WELCOME

HOW TO USE THIS JOURNAL

To start you off nice and easy, this journal has a page for you to fill in everything about you. How you read at least – sorry but that's all we care about here. It will help you work out what kind of reader you are, how you like to read, and what you like to read as you work through filling in these first pages to make sure you can make the best of the free time you save to dive into a new book.

Whether you're part of a book club, online community or just flying solo, you can keep track of how much you want to read, help you set new goals and, better still, actually meet them. We even have a page for you to keep track of all the titles thrown your way to add to your TBR (to be read) pile instead of keeping them in various documents, on scraps of paper around the house, or – worst of all – just hoping you'll remember them. And, just as important as the books you have read, the book you DNF (did not finish) so you don't keep picking them up and trying again.

Then we have the pages for the actual books, of course. Once you finish a book (or as you go if something on the page screams out as important enough that you just need to take note of it straight away) let the prompts guide you through what you need to remember about the book. The story doesn't end when we finish the last page, it lingers in your mind, and now you'll have the perfect way to revisit it or share it with your friends.

4

Lastly, we have activities at the end of the book for you to compare everything you've read. Read these first and keep them in mind whenever you pick up your book. They're here to steal the best moments to help you find your perfect style of book or at least help you with the conversation to get there. If nothing else, they can be great fun to see how all of your books and reading style go together.

So, if you think you've got the gist of it, have a quick read through the journal, learn the pages, then get ready to dive into your next read!

ALL
ABOUT
YOU

ALL ABOUT YOU

NAME:

CURRENT READING LOCATION:

FAVOURITE GENRE(S):

TOP FIVE BOOKS OF ALL TIME:

1.

2.

3.

4.

5.

FAVOURITE PLACE(S) TO READ:

BACKGROUND NOISE OR SILENCE WHEN READING:

AUTHOR LIVING OR DEAD YOU'D MOST LIKE TO MEET:

ALL ABOUT YOU

YOUR READING STYLE

What kind of reader are you? Colour the iris of the eye (or eyes) that best correspond to your reading style/s.

INTENSIVE READER

You disappear into the world of whatever it is you're reading, completely disconnecting from reality, re-emerging to find hours have passed without you even realising.

EXTENSIVE READER

Volume, baby! You like to read in copious amounts, and your TBR list often hits over 100 books a year.

HOLIDAY READER

You exclusively read when you're relaxing on a getaway. It's like your second personality.

LATE NIGHT READER

A night owl, you like to reserve reading for once the day is over. Often in bed and in your pyjamas.

You read when you want! There's no rhyme or reason for when you pick up a book, it just depends on how you feel that day, month, year . . .

Train to catch each day? Long plane ride ahead? No worries, you'll bring a book! You like to read while in transit to help pass the time. Or maybe that's the only time you get to yourself . . .

You like to read quickly and get the gist of a book without wasting time. You often miss key plot lines, but whatever.

You have a set time every day or week that you allocate to reading. You are most likely someone who is very organised and has good boundaries.

This category is reserved exclusively for those who work in publishing. You read manuscripts for work, not for fun. Most of the time your brain is done with reading when it comes time to relax.

TBR (TO BE READ)

So many books, so little free time.

It seems like most TBR piles grow at about double the rate they get worked through, so this section will probably never be empty. But it's good to keep track of the titles you come across (or are thrown at you) that you simply *must* read one day.

ALL ABOUT YOU

READING GOALS TRACKER

Let's see how much you're actually reading at a glance. Colour in a spine for each day you read on your 365-day challenge. If you skip a day then colour it in black, it's okay to have some darker books on your shelf . . . we don't judge.

ALL ABOUT YOU

| JAN |
| FEB |
| MAR |
| APR |
| MAY |
| JUN |
| JUL |
| AUG |
| SEP |
| OCT |
| NOV |
| DEC |

DNF (DID NOT FINISH)

Maybe the writing style just isn't flowing for you, or maybe a main character has hit on one of your 'icks' and you just can't move on. Whatever the reason that's stopped you reading, now's the time to put it down and make a quick note of what stopped you so you can steer clear in the future.

It's okay, there are a few other books out there in the world. We'll find the right ones for you.

DNF

MOSTLY HERE FOR THE SMUT

MOSTLY HERE FOR THE SMUT

ROMANTASY AND SMUT

Romantasy has been labelled the hottest hybrid genre for a few years now, so let's break down exactly what that means. Without going all dictionary definition on you here, basically romantasy is the genre that straddles the line of romance and fantasy. Clever, right?

Romantasy as a term might be a newish genre, but it's quickly gained the love and attention it deserves. We get the escapism, magic, high stakes and desperate adventure so common in fantasy writing and then, since our hearts are already pounding, why not fall in love too? *Desperately*.

There are no hard rules for the genre. Sometimes the fantasy is barely there, just a creature that we don't have in the real world, or the whisper of something a little beyond our reality. And sometimes it's the hinge of the whole book, thrown into the middle of a whole other world with a fully-fledged magic system that ties the whole thing together. Same for romance; sometimes it's there (in the background, hinted at, confirmed) but you could still make a story if it was taken out, and sometimes it's EVERYTHING. The world on the pages wouldn't even turn if it wasn't for the characters' love.

The important thing is that the book as it is wouldn't work if it didn't have elements of both genres. From there, you just have to find the balance that works for you. How much of each depends on the author, so if you read a few with different balances you'll be sure to find your sweet spot.

This journal is dedicated to romantasy readers, but, more than that, it's for people who are mostly here for the smut. If you've picked up this book with the word 'smut' in all caps proudly displayed on the cover then hopefully you know what you're getting into. If you have no clue then … oops … but also, let me help you out.

The word 'smut' has been around for a while, and for a good reason. Who isn't drawn to peek behind the door? The word comes from the 16th-century meaning to smudge or blacken. That was slowly corrupted until the 'dirtiness' of the word meant it started to be used in place of something indecent or obscene. Or – for our purposes – writing sexy scenes.

It used to be that anyone reading these kinds of *dirty* books would keep them at home, hidden away, or buy a fake cover for them if they wanted to read in public. But we're past that. Not only can we proudly declare that we're reading smut and we enjoy it, but we even discuss and compare the smut we've read. The only thing you have to do now is actually read it. So go on!

Enjoy!

MOSTLY HERE FOR THE SMUT

TOP 50 ROMANTASY BOOKS

These are the key books, new and 'classic' (since romantasy became a thing, so . . . max 10 years if we backdate) that have the most reads and ratings as voted by readers. Only the first book of a series is listed (if it's part of one), so we have some authors other than Sarah J. Maas, and in no particular order:

- ☐ 1. *The Fourth Wing*, 'The Empyrean' series by Rebecca Yarros (2023)

- ☐ 2. *A Court of Thorns and Roses*, 'A Court of Thorns and Roses' series by Sarah J. Maas (2015)

- ☐ 3. *The Serpent and the Wings of Night*, 'Crowns of Nyaxia' series by Carissa Broadbent (2022)

- ☐ 4. *From Blood and Ash*, 'Blood and Ash' series by Jennifer L. Armentrout (2020)

- ☐ 5. *Powerless*, 'The Powerless Trilogy' by Lauren Roberts (2023)

- ☐ 6. *House of Earth and Blood*, 'Crescent City' series by Sarah J. Maas (2020)

- ☐ 7. *Divine Rivals*, 'Letters of Enchantment' series by Rebecca Ross (2023)

- [ ] 8. *Throne of Glass*, 'Throne of Glass' series by Sarah J. Maas (2012)

- [ ] 9. *Once Upon a Broken Heart*, 'Once Upon a Broken Heart' series by Stephanie Garber (2021)

- [ ] 10. *The Cruel Prince*, 'The Folk of the Air' series by Holly Black (2018)

- [ ] 11. *Bride* by Ali Hazelwood (2024)

- [ ] 12. *One Dark Window*, 'The Shepherd King' series by Rachel Gillig (2022)

- [ ] 13. *A Fate Inked in Blood*, 'Saga of the Unfated' series by Danielle L. Jensen (2024)

- [ ] 14. *When the Moon Hatched*, 'Moonfall' series by Sarah A. Parker (2024)

- [ ] 15. *The Bridge Kingdom*, 'The Bridge Kingdom' series by Danielle L. Jensen (2018)

- [ ] 16. *Daughter of No Worlds*, 'The War of Lost Hearts' series by Carissa Broadbent (2020)

- [ ] 17. *Gild*, 'The Plated Prisoner' series by Raven Kennedy (2020)

- [ ] 18. *Caraval*, 'Caraval' series by Stephanie Garber (2016)

- [ ] 19. *The Crimson Moth*, 'The Crimson Moth' series by Kristen Ciccarelli (2024)

- [ ] 20. *A Shadow in the Ember*, 'Flesh and Fire' series by Jennifer L. Armentrout (2021)

- [ ] 21. *Kingdom of the Wicked*, 'Kingdom of the Wicked' series by Kerri Maniscalco (2020)

- [ ] 22. *A Touch of Darkness*, 'Hades X Persephone Saga' by Scarlett St. Clair (2019)

MOSTLY HERE FOR THE SMUT

☐ 23. *Spark of the Everflame*, 'The Kindred's Curse Saga' by Penn Cole (2023)

☐ 24. *The Book of Azrael*, 'Gods & Monsters' series by Amber V. Nicole (2022)

☐ 25. *Throne of the Fallen*, 'Prince of Sin' series by Kerri Maniscalco (2023)

☐ 26. *A Dawn of Onyx,* 'The Sacred Stones' series by Kate Golden (2022)

☐ 27. *A Court This Cruel and Lovely*, 'Kingdom of Lies' series by Stacia Stark (2023)

☐ 28. *Assistant to the Villain*, 'Assistant and the Villain' by Hannah Nicole Maehrer (2023)

☐ 29. *Zodiac Academy: The Awakening*, 'Zodiac Academy' series by Caroline Peckham and Susanne Valenti (2019)

☐ 30. *The Hurricane Wars*, 'The Hurricane Wars' series by Thea Guanzon (2023)

☐ 31. *The Hanging City* by Charlie N. Holmberg (2023)

☐ 32. *The Jasad Heir*, 'The Scorched Throne' series by Sara Hashem (2023)

☐ 33. *The Elf Tangent* by Lindsay Buroker (2022)

☐ 34. *Bound to the Dark Elf King*, 'Of Fate and Kings' series by Jessica Grayson (2022)

☐ 35. *The Masked Fae*, 'Royal Fae of Rose Briar Woods' series by Shari L. Tapscott (2022)

☐ 36. *What Lies Beyond the Veil*, 'Of Flesh and Bone' series by Harper L. Woods (2022)

☐ 37. *Bride of the Shadow King*, 'Bride of the Shadow King' series by Sylvia Mercedes (2022)

☐ 38. *Bride to the Fiend Prince*, 'Dark Rulers' series
by Rebecca F. Kenney (2021)

☐ 39. *River of Shadows*, 'Underworld Gods' series
by Karina Halle (2022)

☐ 40. *City of Gods and Monsters*, 'House of Devils'
series by Kayla Edwards (2022)

☐ 41. *Midnight Moon*, 'Rebel Wolf' series by Linsey Hall
(2022)

☐ 42. *Ravaged by Monsters*, 'Dark Temptations' series
by Katie May and Ann Denton (2022)

☐ 43. *Legendborn*, 'The Legendborn Cycle' series
by Tracy Deonn (2020)

☐ 44. *The Witch Collector*, 'Witch Walker' series
by Charissa Weaks (2021)

☐ 45. *Trial of the Sun Queen*, 'Artefacts of Ouranos'
series by Nisha J. Tuli (2023)

☐ 46. *A River of Golden Bones*, 'The Golden Court'
series by A.K. Mulford (2023)

☐ 47. *That Time I Got Drunk and Saved a Demon*, 'Mead
Mishaps' series by Kimberly Lemming (2021)

☐ 48. *King of Battle and Blood*, 'Adrian X Isolde'
series by Scarlett St. Clair (2021)

☐ 49. *A Strange and Stubborn Endurance*, 'The Tithenai
Chronicles' series by Foz Meadows (2022)

☐ 50. *A Broken Blade*, 'The Halfling Saga'
by Melissa Blair (2021)

MOSTLY HERE FOR THE SMUT

YOUR TOP *10* ROMANTASY BOOKS

1.

2.

3.

4.

5.

6.

7.

8.

9.

10.

MOSTLY HERE FOR THE SMUT

READING LOG

READING LOG

BOOK NUMBER _____

TITLE: _____

AUTHOR: _____

GENRE: _____

FORMAT:

◯ Hardback ◯ Paperback ◯ Ebook ◯ Audio

STARTED ON: _____

FINISHED ON: _____

INITIAL THOUGHTS: _____

MY RATINGS

PLOT

WRITING

CHARACTERS

OVERALL

READING LOG

READING LOG

MY THOUGHTS:

MY THOUGHTS:

READING LOG

READING LOG

MY THOUGHTS:

MY THOUGHTS:

READING LOG

READING LOG

BOOK CLUB NOTES: _____

BOOK CLUB NOTES:

READING LOG

BOOK CLUB NOTES: _____

BOOK CLUB NOTES: _____

READING LOG

BOOK NUMBER _____

TITLE: _____

AUTHOR: _____

GENRE: _____

FORMAT:

○ Hardback ○ Paperback ○ Ebook ○ Audio

STARTED ON: _____

FINISHED ON: _____

INITIAL THOUGHTS: _____

MY RATINGS

PLOT

WRITING

CHARACTERS

OVERALL

MY THOUGHTS:

MY THOUGHTS:

READING LOG

READING LOG

MY THOUGHTS: _____

MY THOUGHTS:

READING LOG

BOOK CLUB NOTES:

BOOK CLUB NOTES:

READING LOG

BOOK CLUB NOTES: _____

BOOK CLUB NOTES:

READING LOG

READING LOG

BOOK NUMBER _____

TITLE: _____

AUTHOR: _____

GENRE: _____

FORMAT:

◯ Hardback   ◯ Paperback   ◯ Ebook   ◯ Audio

STARTED ON: _____

FINISHED ON: _____

INITIAL THOUGHTS: _____

_____

_____

_____

_____

_____

_____

_____

MY RATINGS

PLOT

WRITING

CHARACTERS

OVERALL

READING LOG

MY THOUGHTS:

MY THOUGHTS:

READING LOG

MY THOUGHTS:

MY THOUGHTS:

READING LOG

READING LOG

BOOK CLUB NOTES: _____

BOOK CLUB NOTES: _____

READING LOG

BOOK CLUB NOTES: _____

BOOK CLUB NOTES: _____

READING LOG

READING LOG

BOOK NUMBER _____

TITLE: _____

AUTHOR: _____

GENRE: _____

FORMAT:

⬡ Hardback   ⬡ Paperback   ⬡ Ebook   ⬡ Audio

STARTED ON: _____

FINISHED ON: _____

INITIAL THOUGHTS: _____

_____

_____

_____

_____

_____

_____

_____

MY RATINGS

PLOT

WRITING

CHARACTERS

OVERALL

READING LOG

MY THOUGHTS:

MY THOUGHTS:

READING LOG

MY THOUGHTS:

MY THOUGHTS:

READING LOG

READING LOG

BOOK CLUB NOTES: _____

BOOK CLUB NOTES:

READING LOG

READING LOG

BOOK CLUB NOTES: _____

BOOK CLUB NOTES:

READING LOG

READING LOG

BOOK NUMBER _____

TITLE: _____

AUTHOR: _____

GENRE: _____

FORMAT:

◯ Hardback   ◯ Paperback   ◯ Ebook   ◯ Audio

STARTED ON: _____

FINISHED ON: _____

INITIAL THOUGHTS: _____

_____

_____

_____

_____

_____

_____

_____

MY RATINGS

PLOT

WRITING

CHARACTERS

OVERALL

READING LOG

MY THOUGHTS:

MY THOUGHTS:

READING LOG

MY THOUGHTS:

MY THOUGHTS:

READING LOG

READING LOG

BOOK CLUB NOTES:

BOOK CLUB NOTES:

READING LOG

BOOK CLUB NOTES: _____

BOOK CLUB NOTES:

READING LOG

BOOK NUMBER _____

TITLE: _____

AUTHOR: _____

GENRE: _____

FORMAT:

◯ Hardback   ◯ Paperback   ◯ Ebook   ◯ Audio

STARTED ON: _____

FINISHED ON: _____

INITIAL THOUGHTS: _____

_____

_____

_____

_____

_____

_____

_____

MY RATINGS

PLOT

WRITING

CHARACTERS

OVERALL

READING LOG

MY THOUGHTS:

MY THOUGHTS:

READING LOG

READING LOG

MY THOUGHTS:

MY THOUGHTS:

READING LOG

BOOK CLUB NOTES: _____

BOOK CLUB NOTES:

READING LOG

READING LOG

BOOK CLUB NOTES: _____

BOOK CLUB NOTES:

READING LOG

BOOK NUMBER _____

TITLE: _____

AUTHOR: _____

GENRE: _____

FORMAT:

○ Hardback   ○ Paperback   ○ Ebook   ○ Audio

STARTED ON: _____

FINISHED ON: _____

INITIAL THOUGHTS: _____

_____

_____

_____

_____

_____

_____

_____

MY RATINGS

PLOT

WRITING

CHARACTERS

OVERALL

READING LOG

MY THOUGHTS:

MY THOUGHTS:

READING LOG

READING LOG

MY THOUGHTS:

MY THOUGHTS:

READING LOG

READING LOG

BOOK CLUB NOTES: _____

BOOK CLUB NOTES:

READING LOG

BOOK CLUB NOTES: _____

BOOK CLUB NOTES:

READING LOG

BOOK NUMBER _____

TITLE: _____

AUTHOR: _____

GENRE: _____

FORMAT:

○ Hardback ○ Paperback ○ Ebook ○ Audio

STARTED ON: _____

FINISHED ON: _____

INITIAL THOUGHTS: _____

_____

_____

_____

_____

_____

_____

_____

MY RATINGS

PLOT

WRITING

CHARACTERS

OVERALL

READING LOG

MY THOUGHTS: _____

MY THOUGHTS:

READING LOG

READING LOG

MY THOUGHTS:

MY THOUGHTS:

READING LOG

READING LOG

BOOK CLUB NOTES: _____

BOOK CLUB NOTES:

READING LOG

READING LOG

BOOK CLUB NOTES: _____

BOOK CLUB NOTES:

READING LOG

BOOK NUMBER _____

TITLE: _____

AUTHOR: _____

GENRE: _____

FORMAT:

◯ Hardback   ◯ Paperback   ◯ Ebook   ◯ Audio

STARTED ON: _____

FINISHED ON: _____

INITIAL THOUGHTS: _____

_____

_____

_____

_____

_____

_____

_____

MY RATINGS

PLOT

WRITING

CHARACTERS

OVERALL

READING LOG

MY THOUGHTS:

MY THOUGHTS:

READING LOG

MY THOUGHTS: _____

MY THOUGHTS:

READING LOG

READING LOG

BOOK CLUB NOTES: _____

BOOK CLUB NOTES:

READING LOG

BOOK CLUB NOTES:

BOOK CLUB NOTES:

READING LOG

READING LOG

BOOK NUMBER _____

TITLE:_____

AUTHOR:_____

GENRE:_____

FORMAT:

◯ Hardback   ◯ Paperback   ◯ Ebook   ◯ Audio

STARTED ON:_____

FINISHED ON:_____

INITIAL THOUGHTS:_____

MY RATINGS

PLOT

WRITING

CHARACTERS

OVERALL

READING LOG

READING LOG

MY THOUGHTS:

MY THOUGHTS:

READING LOG

READING LOG

MY THOUGHTS:

MY THOUGHTS:

READING LOG

READING LOG

BOOK CLUB NOTES: _____

BOOK CLUB NOTES:

READING LOG

BOOK CLUB NOTES: _____

BOOK CLUB NOTES:

READING LOG

BOOK NUMBER _____

TITLE: _____

AUTHOR: _____

GENRE: _____

FORMAT:

◯ Hardback   ◯ Paperback   ◯ Ebook   ◯ Audio

STARTED ON: _____

FINISHED ON: _____

INITIAL THOUGHTS: _____

_____

_____

_____

_____

_____

_____

_____

MY RATINGS

PLOT

WRITING

CHARACTERS

OVERALL

READING LOG

MY THOUGHTS:

MY THOUGHTS:

MY THOUGHTS:

MY THOUGHTS:

READING LOG

READING LOG

BOOK CLUB NOTES: _____

BOOK CLUB NOTES:

READING LOG

BOOK CLUB NOTES: _____

BOOK CLUB NOTES:

READING LOG

READING LOG

BOOK NUMBER _____

TITLE: _____

AUTHOR: _____

GENRE: _____

FORMAT:

◯ Hardback   ◯ Paperback   ◯ Ebook   ◯ Audio

STARTED ON: _____

FINISHED ON: _____

INITIAL THOUGHTS: _____

_____

_____

_____

_____

_____

_____

_____

MY RATINGS

PLOT

WRITING

CHARACTERS

OVERALL

READING LOG

READING LOG

MY THOUGHTS:

MY THOUGHTS:

READING LOG

READING LOG

MY THOUGHTS:

MY THOUGHTS:

READING LOG

BOOK CLUB NOTES: _____

BOOK CLUB NOTES:

READING LOG

BOOK CLUB NOTES: _____

BOOK CLUB NOTES: _____

READING LOG

BOOK NUMBER _____

TITLE: _____

AUTHOR: _____

GENRE: _____

FORMAT:

◯ Hardback   ◯ Paperback   ◯ Ebook   ◯ Audio

STARTED ON: _____

FINISHED ON: _____

INITIAL THOUGHTS: _____

MY RATINGS

PLOT

WRITING

CHARACTERS

OVERALL

READING LOG

MY THOUGHTS:

MY THOUGHTS:

READING LOG

MY THOUGHTS: _____

MY THOUGHTS:

READING LOG

BOOK CLUB NOTES: _____

BOOK CLUB NOTES:

READING LOG

BOOK CLUB NOTES: _____

BOOK CLUB NOTES:

READING LOG

BOOK NUMBER _____

TITLE: _____

AUTHOR: _____

GENRE: _____

FORMAT:

◯ Hardback　　◯ Paperback　　◯ Ebook　　◯ Audio

STARTED ON: _____

FINISHED ON: _____

INITIAL THOUGHTS: _____

_____

_____

_____

_____

_____

_____

MY RATINGS

PLOT

WRITING

CHARACTERS

OVERALL

READING LOG

MY THOUGHTS:

MY THOUGHTS:

READING LOG

MY THOUGHTS:

MY THOUGHTS:

READING LOG

READING LOG

BOOK CLUB NOTES: _____

BOOK CLUB NOTES:

READING LOG

BOOK CLUB NOTES: _____

BOOK CLUB NOTES:

READING LOG

BOOK NUMBER _____

TITLE: _____

AUTHOR: _____

GENRE: _____

FORMAT:

○ Hardback ○ Paperback ○ Ebook ○ Audio

STARTED ON: _____

FINISHED ON: _____

INITIAL THOUGHTS: _____

_____

_____

_____

_____

_____

_____

_____

MY RATINGS

PLOT

WRITING

CHARACTERS

OVERALL

READING LOG

MY THOUGHTS:

MY THOUGHTS:

READING LOG

MY THOUGHTS:

MY THOUGHTS:

READING LOG

BOOK CLUB NOTES: _____

BOOK CLUB NOTES:

READING LOG

BOOK CLUB NOTES: _____

BOOK CLUB NOTES:

READING LOG

BOOK NUMBER _____

TITLE: _____

AUTHOR: _____

GENRE: _____

FORMAT:

◯ Hardback ◯ Paperback ◯ Ebook ◯ Audio

STARTED ON: _____

FINISHED ON: _____

INITIAL THOUGHTS: _____

_____

_____

_____

_____

_____

_____

MY RATINGS

PLOT

WRITING

CHARACTERS

OVERALL

READING LOG

READING LOG

MY THOUGHTS: _____

MY THOUGHTS:

READING LOG

MY THOUGHTS:

MY THOUGHTS:

READING LOG

BOOK CLUB NOTES: _____

BOOK CLUB NOTES:

READING LOG

READING LOG

BOOK CLUB NOTES: _____

BOOK CLUB NOTES:

READING LOG

BOOK NUMBER _____

TITLE: _____

AUTHOR: _____

GENRE: _____

FORMAT:

◯ Hardback ◯ Paperback ◯ Ebook ◯ Audio

STARTED ON: _____

FINISHED ON: _____

INITIAL THOUGHTS: _____

_____

_____

_____

_____

_____

_____

_____

MY RATINGS

PLOT

WRITING

CHARACTERS

OVERALL

READING LOG

MY THOUGHTS:

MY THOUGHTS:

READING LOG

READING LOG

MY THOUGHTS:

MY THOUGHTS:

READING LOG

BOOK CLUB NOTES:

BOOK CLUB NOTES:

READING LOG

BOOK CLUB NOTES:

BOOK CLUB NOTES:

ACTIVITIES

ACTIVITIES

ALL COVERED

Sketch your favourite covers from the books you've read this year.

ACTIVITIES

ACTIVITIES

ACTIVITIES

ACTIVITIES

SPICE METER

HOW SPICY DO YOU LIKE YOUR ROMANCE?

Colour the thermometer to match your preferred spice level.

MOLTEN
Reserved for when there are pages that strike you as almost PWP (porn without plot). Probably with a handful of kinks thrown in for good measure.

BURNING
Now we're getting graphic, nothing held back. We're seeing the whole scene.

HOT
Here we're seeing the good stuff, not all the details. More feelings than touch by touch, but his pants are open.

STEAMY
Something's *definitely* going on, but it just fades out before we get anything too NSFW.

WARM
There's attraction and kissing, but no real action here. Just all the feels.

SPICE METER

WHERE DO YOUR READS RANK?
Rank your reads on the spice scale below.

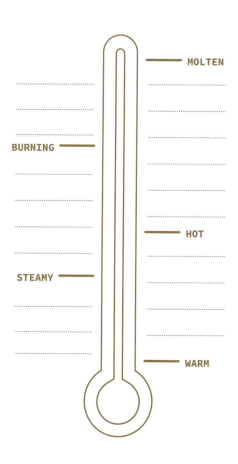

MOLTEN

BURNING

HOT

STEAMY

WARM

ACTIVITIES

ACTIVITIES

PICK YOUR POISON

Give each trope a score out of 10 on what works for you. This is a great page to snap and share to get new recommendations. As you make your way through your TBR pile, check back in with this list to make sure it's still tracking. If you rated 10/10 for ETL (enemies to lovers) but *The Cruel Prince* by Holly Black wasn't your vibe, you might want to rethink your scores.

THE TROPES

ENEMIES TO LOVERS /10

FORBIDDEN LOVE /10

FRIENDS TO LOVERS /10

FAKE RELATIONSHIP /10

LOVE TRIANGLE /10

SOULMATES /10

SECOND CHANCE ROMANCE /10

FORCED PROXIMITY /10

SECRET IDENTITY /10

ARRANGED MARRIAGE /10

ROYALTY/COMMONER /10

BEAUTY AND THE BEAST /10

OPPOSITES ATTRACT /10

ACTIVITIES

ACTIVITIES

JUST STOP

People love to hate almost as much as they love to love. Whether it's bad writing, wrong timing or a pet peeve, sometimes one action, phrase or word can completely ruin a scene – and sometimes that's hilarious.

Keep a record of your *favourite* mood killers here.

ACTIVITIES

WORST PET NAMES

CRINGIEST SCENES

BAD BODY PART SYNONYMS

ACTIVITIES

ACTIVITIES

BOOK CLUB CONTACT LIST

NAME	NUMBER	EMAIL

BOOK CLUB CONTACT LIST

NAME	NUMBER	EMAIL

A Sweet Hearts Press book
An imprint of Rockpool Publishing
PO Box 252
Summer Hill
NSW 2130 Australia

sweetheartspress.com

Follow us! ◉ sweethearts_press
Tag your images with #sweetheartspress

ISBN: 9781923208278

Published in 2025 by Sweet Hearts Press
Copyright text and design © Sweet Hearts Press 2025

All rights reserved. No part of this publication may be reproduced, stored in a retrieval system, or transmitted in any form or by any means, electronic, mechanical, photocopying, recording or otherwise, without the prior written permission of the publisher.

Written by Kaitlyn Smith
Edited by Candace Stuart

Printed and bound in China
10 9 8 7 6 5 4 3 2 1